THE SOLAR SYSTEM

THE SUN

A MyReportLinks.com Book

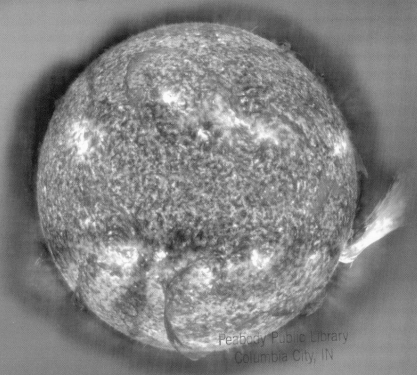

STEPHEN FEINSTEIN

MyReportLinks.com Books

an imprint of

 Enslow Publishers, Inc.

Box 398, 40 Industrial Road
Berkeley Heights, NJ 07922
USA

MyReportLinks.com Books, an imprint of Enslow Publishers, Inc. MyReportLinks®
is a registered trademark of Enslow Publishers, Inc.

Library of Congress Cataloging-in-Publication Data

Feinstein, Stephen.
   The sun / Stephen Feinstein.
      p. cm. — (The solar system)
   Includes bibliographical references and index.
   ISBN 0-7660-5305-9
   1. Sun—Juvenile literature. I. Title. II. Solar system (Berkeley Heights, N.J.)
   QB521.5.F45 2005
   523.7—dc22
                     2004013756

Printed in the United States of America

10 9 8 7 6 5 4 3 2 1

To Our Readers:
Through the purchase of this book, you and your library gain access to the Report Links that specifically back
up this book.
The Publisher will provide access to the Report Links that back up this book and will keep these Report Links
up to date on **www.myreportlinks.com** for five years from the book's first publication date.
We have done our best to make sure all Internet addresses in this book were active and appropriate when we went
to press. However, the author and the Publisher have no control over, and assume no liability for, the material
available on those Internet sites or on other Web sites they may link to.
The usage of the MyReportLinks.com Books Web site is subject to the terms and conditions stated on the Usage
Policy Statement on **www.myreportlinks.com**.
A password may be required to access the Report Links that back up this book. The password is found on the
bottom of page 4 of this book.
Any comments or suggestions can be sent by e-mail to comments@myreportlinks.com or to the address on the
back cover.

Photo Credits: © Corel Corporation, pp. 10, 12, 13, 33; © Nicolaus Copernicus Museum, p. 15; Department
of Physics, University of Nevada, Reno, p. 39; Lunar and Planetary Institute, p. 30; MyReportLinks.com Books,
p. 4; National Aeronautics and Space Administration (NASA), pp. 1, 3, 9, 17, 20, 24, 27, 29, 35, 38, 41;
Photos.com, pp. 3, 9, 26; The Solar and Heliospheric Observatory, pp. 19, 22, 32, 36, 42, 44.

Note: Some NASA photos were only available in a low-resolution format.

Cover Photo: National Aeronautics and Space Administration.

MyReportLinks.com Books
Great Books, Great Links, Great for Research!

The Internet sites listed on the next four pages can save you hours of research time. These Internet sites—we call them "Report Links"—are constantly changing, but we keep them up to date on our Web site.

Give it a try! Type http://www.myreportlinks.com into your browser, click on the series title, then the book title, and scroll down to the Report Links listed for this book.

The Report Links will bring you to great source documents, photographs, and illustrations. MyReportLinks.com Books save you time, feature Report Links that are kept up to date, and make report writing easier than ever!

Please see "To Our Readers" on the copyright page for important information about this book, the MyReportLinks.com Web site, and the Report Links that back up this book.

Please enter **PTS1138** if asked for a password.

Report Links

 The Internet sites described below can be accessed at
http://www.myreportlinks.com

*EDITOR'S CHOICE

▶**Solar System Exploration: Sun**
From NASA comes a helpful overview of the Sun. Measurements
are available in both English and metric notation. Images of the Sun
are included.

*EDITOR'S CHOICE

▶**The Sun: Your Travel Guide to the Solar System**
This BBC space site about the Sun covers some of its physical
characteristics, such as flares, sunspots, solar wind, and temperature,
and discusses how each affects Earth.

*EDITOR'S CHOICE

▶**Nineplanets.org: The Sun**
This site features information on the Sun's outer layers, atmosphere,
solar wind, eclipses, and satellites.

*EDITOR'S CHOICE

▶**NASA's Imagine The Universe!: The Sun**
The Sun has three outer layers that make up its atmosphere: the
photosphere, the chromosphere, and the corona. This site provides a
good overview of each. Links to additional information are provided.

*EDITOR'S CHOICE

▶**StarChild: The Sun**
Learn the basics about the Sun and its properties from this site. A movie
about the Sun is included.

*EDITOR'S CHOICE

▶**National Maritime Museum: The Sun**
Learn more about the Sun from this site. Solar flares, the photosphere,
sunspots, and the solar cycle are discussed. Follow the links to read more
about the Sun.

Report Links

The Internet sites described below can be accessed at
http://www.myreportlinks.com

▶**Ask a Space Scientist About the Sun**

Learn about the celestial Sun from this NASA site, which provides a scientist's answers to commonly asked questions about the Sun.

▶**The Electronic Sky: The Sun**

This site provides the reader with a short history of the Sun, beginning with its protostar stage through to its eventual death as a Black Dwarf.

▶**Equinoxes and Solstices**

From this site, learn how Earth's orbit around the Sun creates our seasons. Information is provided on the solstices, equinoxes, celestial poles, and the ecliptic.

▶**Eye Safety and Solar Eclipses**

When solar eclipses occur, many people want to see and even photograph these natural events. But looking at the Sun directly can cause blindness. At this NASA site, learn how to view the Sun safely.

▶**Famous Astronomers**

This site offers brief biographies of astronomers, beginning with the ancient Greeks and continuing to the present. It also includes images of each astronomer.

▶**Famous Astronomers and Astrophysicists**

Astronomers beginning with Copernicus have changed the way we look at the sky because of their important work regarding the Sun. At this site, read about these great men of science and view images of them.

▶**How the Sun Works**

Learn about the Sun from this seven-part article written by a scientist. There is information on the parts of the Sun, its atmosphere, sunspots, flares, the Sun's surface, and its future. Follow the links to go to the next section.

▶**Layers of the Sun**

Learn about the Sun's layers when you visit this site. Information is available on the core, radiative envelope, convective envelope, photosphere, chromosphere, and corona.

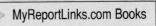
Report Links

The Internet sites described below can be accessed at
http://www.myreportlinks.com

▶**Mystery of Stonehenge Points to the Heavens**

This site takes a look at Stonehenge, an ancient monument made out of standing stones. Read the various theories about who built it and why and how it relates to the Sun.

▶**Myths About the Sun**

The Sun has always played an important role in human culture. This site includes links to eighteen different Sun myths, including those of the Greeks, the Norse, the Aztecs, and the Incas.

▶**Nicolaus Copernicus Museum, Frombork**

The Nicolaus Copernicus Museum in Frombork, Poland, offers an interesting look at the sixteenth-century astronomer who argued convincingly that the Sun is at the center of the solar system.

▶**Our Sun**

Sunspots appear as dark spots on the surface of the Sun in the area of the photosphere. Some are large enough that we can see them from Earth. This site offers a good description of sunspots.

▶**The Singing Sun**

Are you surprised to learn that the Sun is filled with sound? This Stanford University site is a good place to start learning about solar music.

▶**Solar and Heliospheric Observatory**

This site is home to the SOHO project, a joint mission of NASA and the European Space Agency (ESA) to learn more about the Sun. The ESA/NASA solar observatory has an Extreme Ultraviolet Imaging Telescope (EIT) on board to capture images of the Sun.

▶**Solar Eclipse Page**

A solar eclipse can only occur at New Moon when the Moon passes between Earth and the Sun. Learn more about eclipses from this site, and read about the differences between partial and total solar eclipses.

▶**Solar Physics**

Solar physics really began when the telescope was invented in the early 1600s. The quest for a better understanding of our most important star continues. Learn more about solar physics from this NASA site.

Report Links

The Internet sites described below can be accessed at
http://www.myreportlinks.com

▶**Solar Probe**

The Solar Probe mission to the Sun will be the first to visit a star. The objective is to study the Sun's corona and the solar wind that is produced by it. This site is home to NASA's Solar Probe project.

▶**Stanford Solar Center**

The Solar Oscillations Investigation Team at Stanford University is dedicated to making the learning of solar science a fun thing. This site provides some interesting information about the Sun.

▶**STEREO**

A better understanding of coronal mass ejections (CMEs) is important because these eruptions on the Sun's surface cause power surges and communication disruptions on Earth. This site is home to STEREO, a NASA mission planned for 2006 to study CMEs.

▶**Sun**

The Sun is the closest star to Earth, and without it, we would have no light, heat, or life. This site provides information on missions to the Sun, solar statistics, and solar discoveries, and includes images and movies.

▶**The Sun: A Nearby Star**

This site offers a comprehensive study of the Sun, including information on the Sun's physical properties, an explanation of helioseismology, and a look at the Sun's atmosphere, core, magnetic field, basic solar properties, and solar composition.

▶**Sun-Earth Connection**

This NASA site is home to the Sun-Earth Connection program, which studies the Sun and its relationship to Earth. All of the NASA space science missions to the Sun are reviewed.

▶**Sunspots**

Sunspots are dark, irregularly shaped areas on the surface of the Sun. Sunspots appear dark because they are cooler than the surface of the Sun. Learn more about them from this museum site.

▶**Why We Study the Sun**

This NASA site explains why it is important for humans to study the Sun and send missions to our nearest star.

Any comments? Contact us: **comments@myreportlinks.com**

The Sun Facts

Age
About 4.5 billion years

Diameter at Equator
863,700 miles (1,390,000 kilometers)

Composition
About 74 percent hydrogen, 25 percent helium, and
1 percent other elements including oxygen, nitrogen,
carbon, iron, neon, calcium, nickel, and aluminum

Distance From Earth
About 93,000,000 miles (150,000,000 kilometers)

Rotational Period
25 days at equator
35 days at poles

Orbital Period
One trip around galactic center: 240 million years

Temperature
At the surface, or top of photosphere: 10,000°F (5,538°C)
At the core: 27,000,000°F (15,000,000°C)

Sunspot Cycle
Approximately 11 years, but with variations

Volume
1.3 million times larger than Earth

Mass
About 333,000 times more massive than Earth

Chapter 1

The Closest Star

At a distance of about 93 million miles (150 million kilometers), the Sun is far closer to us than any other star. The next nearest star, Proxima Centauri, is 4.2 light-years away. This might not sound like a great distance. But keep in mind that a light-year is nearly 6 trillion miles (9.7 trillion kilometers), the distance light travels in one year at a speed of 186,282 miles per second (299,792 kilometers per second). So Proxima Centauri is very, very far away—more than 25 trillion miles (40 trillion kilometers)—so far that it takes light from that star 4.2 years to reach Earth.

To the naked eye, the Sun seems huge compared to all other stars. But scientists classify our Sun as an ordinary average type of

▲ *The Sun, our closest star, makes life on Earth possible.*

star known as a main sequence star, one of hundreds of billions of stars residing in the Milky Way galaxy. There are many stars in this galaxy that are smaller than the Sun. The galaxy also includes stars that are thousands of times bigger and brighter than the Sun. Some are even one million times as bright as the Sun.[1] But by far the most important star for us on Planet Earth is the Sun. It provides the energy that makes life possible. If the Sun suddenly stopped shining, life could not continue to exist on Earth. And if there had never been a Sun, none of us would have ever lived. The Earth itself would never have come into being.

▶ An Incandescent God

To people of the ancient world, the Sun was anything but ordinary. In those early times, people of course did not yet have scientific knowledge about the Sun or any of the other heavenly bodies. But even so, they did have a strong feeling of just how important the Sun was. They realized that the Sun was a giver of life. And they worshipped the burning incandescent ball of gas in the sky as a god.

Different cultures each had their own version of a Sun god or goddess. The ancient Babylonians worshipped Shamash. The Persians worshipped Mithras. The Greek Sun god was called Helios, while Sol was the Roman god of the Sun. That name is still in use today in the adjective *solar,* used to describe anything having to do with the Sun, such as solar system, solar eclipse, solar flare, and solar energy. The Germans worshipped Sunna, the Sun goddess, from which we get the word *sun.*

In ancient Egypt, the pharaoh Amenhotep IV believed that the Sun was the one and only god, the source of all life. This idea broke with the belief that Egyptians had had for years, that there were many gods. He founded the world's first monotheistic religion, requiring all Egyptians to worship only the Sun god. He changed the name of the Sun god from the traditional Ra or Amon-Ra to Aton and then changed his own name from Amenhotep to Akhenaton, "He Who Is of Service to Aton."

▲ *The ancient Egyptians, like many other ancient cultures, worshiped the Sun as a god.*

In 1360 B.C., Akhenaton wrote a hymn to the Sun:

> Beautiful is your rising in the horizon of heaven, living Sun, you who were first at the beginning of things. You shine in the horizon of the East, you fill every land with your beauty. You are beautiful and great and shining. Your rays embrace the lands to the limits of all that you have made. You are far, but your rays are on the earth. . . . The beings of earth are formed under your hand as you have wanted them. You rise and they live. Their eyes look at your beauty until you set and all work comes to a stop as you set in the West.[2]

Native people of the Americas also worshipped the Sun. Tawa was the Sun god of the Hopi people in what is now the southwestern part of the United States. The Sun god of the Incas in South

America was called Inti. The Aztecs, who lived in what is now Mexico, worshipped a powerful Sun god known as Huitzilopochtli. According to the Aztecs, the Sun god made the Sun rise each morning as long as he received his daily offering of human blood. Otherwise the Sun would fall from the sky, and all life on Earth would die. So the Aztecs believed that Huitzilopochtli required human sacrifice on a massive scale. At the altar atop the pyramid of the Great Temple in the Aztec capital of Tenochtitlán, Aztec priests carved out the hearts of living victims using sharp knives made from obsidian, a dark glass formed from cooling lava. According to Aztec legend, when the pyramid was built, its opening was "celebrated" with the sacrifice of twenty thousand people.

Early Observers of the Sun

Although these different cultures of the ancient world developed their own religious practices and customs, all considered the Sun

▲ *Stonehenge, a fascinating stone circle in southern England, may have functioned as an early solar calendar.*

to be extremely important. People saw a direct relationship between the movements of the Sun and the seasons on Earth. For many, it was especially important to keep track of the Sun so they knew the best times for planting crops. Ancient peoples around the world have left monuments of their efforts to understand the Sun and other heavenly bodies.

Almost five thousand years ago, a group of people in what is now southern England built a circular monument of huge stones known as Stonehenge. Stonehenge may have been a solar calendar. On the longest day of the year, the summer solstice, the Sun probably rose exactly between a 35-ton (32-metric ton) boulder called the Heel Stone and another stone no longer standing. This alignment and others may have enabled people to use Stonehenge to time the beginning of summer and winter.[3]

▶ The Heliocentric Theory

For thousands of years, most people believed that the Sun and all the other heavenly bodies revolved around a stationary Earth. The Egyptians believed that their Sun god sailed across the sky in a boat, sailed through the Underworld each night, and reappeared in the sky the next day. The Greeks and Romans believed their Sun god rode across the sky in a chariot and, like the Egyptian god, journeyed through the Underworld each night. People could not see Earth move, so they believed it was stationary and that it was the center around which everything else revolved. People could not actually feel the movement of Earth rotating on its axis, nor could they feel the motion of Earth orbiting the Sun. So why should they have believed otherwise?

Nevertheless, around 270 B.C., a Greek philosopher named Aristarchus estimated that the Sun was much larger than Earth. He concluded that the Sun was at the center of the solar system and that Earth and the other known planets of the time revolved around the Sun. Aristarchus' heliocentric theory challenged the prevailing geocentric theory. But the geocentric theory would

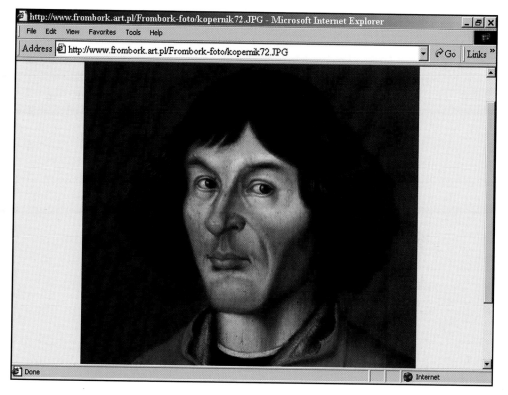

▲ Nicolaus Copernicus' Sun-centered theory of the solar system forever changed human thinking about the universe, which had, for centuries, placed Earth at its center.

remain the commonly accepted understanding of the world for many years.

Other Greek thinkers also tried to determine the actual size and distance of the Sun. But because they based their calculations on incorrect assumptions or inaccurate data, their conclusions were incorrect. Anaxagoras believed that Earth was flat and that the Sun was only 4,000 miles (6,437 kilometers) away. This result then led him to conclude that the Sun, with a diameter of 35 miles (56 kilometers), was much smaller than Earth. Hipparchus studied the timing of solar and lunar eclipses. Based on his observations, he calculated that the Sun was thirty-seven times farther away from us than the Moon and that it was twelve times larger than Earth.

In the second century A.D., the Greek astronomer Ptolemy wrote a complex, detailed description of a geocentric universe that reinforced the prevailing beliefs. His views went mostly unchallenged until the year 1543, when a Polish astronomer named Nicolaus Copernicus revived and expanded upon the heliocentric ideas of Aristarchus in his book *On the Revolutions of the Heavenly Spheres.* Copernicus argued that the Sun is the center of planetary motions. His evidence was so convincing that he brought about a revolution in astronomical science.

The German astronomer Johannes Kepler was a strong believer in Copernicus' heliocentric views. In 1600, Kepler was hired as the assistant to a Danish astronomer named Tycho Brahe. Brahe had made observations over a twenty-year period that supported Copernicus' heliocentric theory. In later years, Kepler, using Brahe's earlier work, discovered that the planets, including Earth, move around the Sun in elliptical orbits rather than in perfect circles. He also discovered that planets move fastest when they are closest to the Sun in their orbital journeys. Since Kepler's time, scientists have continued to study the Sun. They have developed a better understanding of the closest star to Earth—the star that makes life on Earth possible.

A Gigantic Nuclear Furnace

The Sun is an enormous incandescent ball of gas. It has a diameter of 863,700 miles (1,390,000 kilometers), more than 100 times larger than the diameter of Earth. More than 1.3 million Earths could fit inside the Sun. This huge nuclear furnace is hotter than anything we can imagine. The Sun's surface temperature

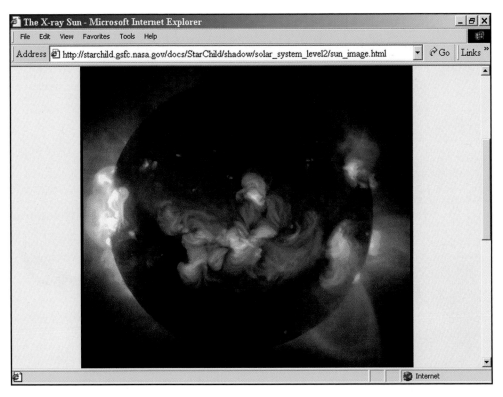

The X-ray Sun - Microsoft Internet Explorer

File   Edit   View   Favorites   Tools   Help

Address http://starchild.gsfc.nasa.gov/docs/StarChild/shadow/solar_system_level2/sun_image.html   Go   Links

Internet

△ This image of the Sun was recorded by a special camera aboard the Yokhoh, a Japanese satellite launched in 1991 to study the X-rays and gamma rays given off by the Sun. (Yokhoh is Japanese for "sunbeam.") The bright areas are places where the very hot gases of the corona are trapped.

is 10,000°F (5,538°C), and the temperature in the Sun's core is an incredible 27,000,000°F (15,000,000°C).

About 74 percent of the Sun is hydrogen, and about 25 percent is helium. Scientists have also detected oxygen, nitrogen, carbon, iron, neon, calcium, nickel, and aluminum. Energy is produced when at high temperatures the hydrogen changes into helium. This occurs through a process called thermonuclear fusion that takes place in the Sun's core.

The fusion process can proceed because the gravitational force of the Sun's mass presses inward on the Sun's core.[1] The nuclei, or central parts, of four hydrogen atoms fuse together to become the nucleus of a single helium atom, releasing energy. This same process in a hydrogen bomb results in a thermonuclear explosion. So in a sense, the Sun's core is a nonstop hydrogen-bomb explosion. Every second, tens of trillions of these reactions take place in the Sun, and 600 million tons (545 million metric tons) of hydrogen become 596 million tons (541 metric tons) of helium. The remaining 4 million tons (3.6 million metric tons) of mass are converted to energy.

▶ The Sun's Incredible Energy

This process in the Sun has been occurring for billions of years and will continue for billions of years into the future. Every second, the Sun gives off enough energy to provide all of Earth's energy needs for five thousand years.[2] More than half of the Sun's energy radiates into space as visible light, which we call sunlight. The rest of the Sun's energy output consists of mostly infrared radiation, ultraviolet radiation, X-rays, and gamma rays. These are all part of the electromagnetic spectrum, which consists of types of radiation, or particles in waves of energy that travel and spread out. Infrared and visible radiation heat our skin, and ultra-violet radiation can heat it too much, causing sunburn. Earth absorbs just a tiny fraction of the Sun's energy, about one billionth of it.[3] And of course, we could not exist without it.

▷ The Sun's Structure

The Sun's core, the intensely hot center where energy is released, is about as big as the planet Jupiter, about 100,000 miles (160,900 kilometers) across. This may seem huge, but the core is actually a relatively small part of the Sun. Because of the tremendous weight bearing down on the core, the hydrogen gas there is extremely dense, about eight times denser than gold. Amazingly, the enormous amount of energy released in the core by fusion each second takes up to, on average, one hundred thousand years to work its way up toward the Sun's surface. There the energy emerges mainly in the form of visible light and infrared radiation. The outward pressure of expanding gas from the core balances the

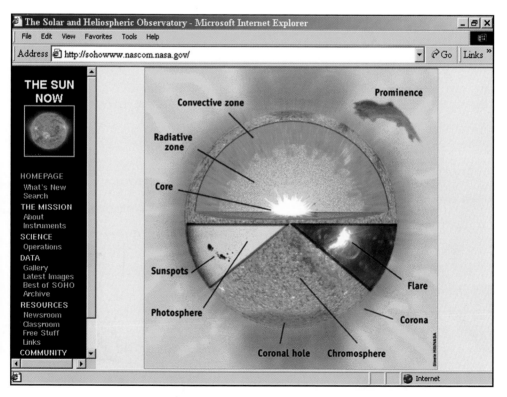

▲ The Sun is broken down into its parts in this diagram. The flare, sunspots, photosphere, chromosphere, and prominence all come from actual images taken by a telescope on board the Solar and Heliospheric Observatory (SOHO), a mission launched in 1995 to study the Sun.

gravitational forces pressing the Sun's mass inward. This prevents the Sun from collapsing under its own weight.

Surrounding the core, where energy is produced, is a region or layer called the radiative zone. Outside the radiative zone is a region or layer called the convective zone, which extends to the Sun's visible surface. Most of the interior of the Sun consists of these two layers. Gamma rays passing through these zones are repeatedly scattered and converted to X-rays and then to ultraviolet rays. The energy particles from the core scatter outward through the radiative zone, a relatively quiet layer. In the convective zone, the outer third of the Sun's interior, the energy is conveyed upward by convection, in which heated gases rise.

The Photosphere

The visible surface of the Sun is called the photosphere. It is a very thin layer of gas, about three hundred miles (five hundred kilometers) deep. Compared to the interior regions of the Sun, it is relatively cool, with a temperature of 10,000°F (5,538°C). Of course, the Sun does not really have a surface, in the sense of solid land or liquid sea. If it were possible for you to land on the Sun's surface, you would rapidly sink because there would be nothing to support your weight. If we think of the photosphere as the

◁ This colorized image of the Sun taken by a satellite looks across the edge of the Sun's surface. The temperature at the surface is "relatively" cool: a mere 10,832°F (6,000°C). But the glowing-red plasma loops (the basic structural elements of the corona) seen rising here from the surface are about 1 million°F (555,538°C).

Sun's surface, then the two layers above it can be considered the Sun's atmosphere. The difference between the Sun's surface and its atmosphere is that the gas is dense and opaque at the surface while it is thin and transparent above the surface.[4]

The Chromosphere and Corona

Above the photosphere is the chromosphere, another relatively thin layer of gases. The chromosphere, which means "color sphere," has a fiery reddish color and is 600 miles (965 kilometers) thick. The lower part of this layer has a temperature of 7,200°F (3,982°C) while the temperature of the upper levels rises to about 18,000°F (9,982°C). The reddish color of the chromosphere is caused by red wavelengths given off by hydrogen atoms when they are heated.[5] The Sun's chromosphere becomes visible to us during a total solar eclipse, when the Moon passes in front of the Sun and completely blocks its face from our view.

Above the chromosphere is the corona ("crown"), the outer atmosphere of the Sun. The temperature of the corona is much higher than that of the chromosphere, rising close to 3,600,000°F (2,000,000°C). Between these two layers is a very thin layer known as the transition region. Here, temperatures rise abruptly from 18,000°F to 1,000,000°F (9,982°C to 555,538°C). Why these temperatures rise is a great mystery, since temperatures would be expected to fall rather than rise at greater distances from the Sun's core. Scientists think that the high temperatures may be caused by gas interacting with strong magnetic fields. Like the chromosphere, the corona can be seen during a total solar eclipse. It appears as a halo or pale white crown of light around the Sun.

The corona extends outward into space for many millions of miles. Beyond about 2 million miles (3 million kilometers), the corona becomes so thin that it is no longer visible. However, the corona actually extends as far from the Sun as Earth and beyond, and scientists can measure it in the form of the solar wind. The solar wind consists of a constant outflow of ionized gas—a stream

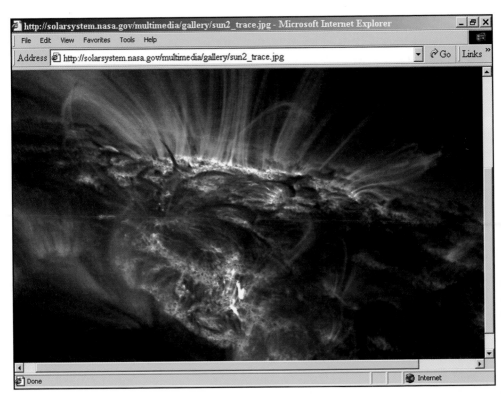

http://solarsystem.nasa.gov/multimedia/gallery/sun2_trace.jpg - Microsoft Internet Explorer

File   Edit   View   Favorites   Tools   Help

Address   http://solarsystem.nasa.gov/multimedia/gallery/sun2_trace.jpg   Go   Links

Done   Internet

△ This ultraviolet image shows glowing arcs of gas encircling sunspots, dark areas on the Sun that are the result of magnetic disturbances.

of charged particles, mainly protons, electrons, and helium nuclei—that is given off by the Sun and sweeps the solar system in all directions at a speed of about 1 million miles per hour (1.6 million kilometers per hour).

▷ Sunspots and Prominences

The Sun is an incredibly stormy place of violent eruptions and clashing magnetic forces. Scientists believe that various magnetic fields have their beginnings in the churning gases in the Sun's interior. Magnetic fields are carried to the surface by rising columns of ionized gas, each about 600 miles (965 kilometers) wide. The gas does not reach the surface in a single smooth journey but rises and falls back many times. As it does, the lines of magnetic force are twisted and coiled. All across the Sun's surface, flickering lights called granules indicate where the 600-mile-wide (965-kilometer-wide) columns of gas have reached the photosphere.

There are also dark spots that appear on the Sun's surface from time to time. These dark spots are enormous magnetic disturbances known as sunspots. Some are as large as 80,000 miles (128,748 kilometers) across, about ten times larger than Earth. Sunspots happen

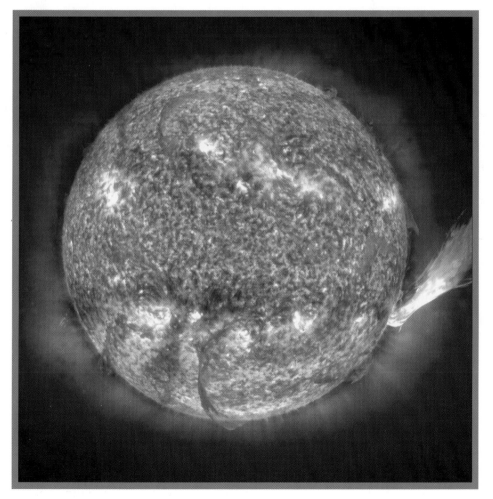

▲ *Solar flares, like the one seen erupting from the Sun in this photograph, may last for just a few minutes but release a tremendous amount of energy in a very short time.*

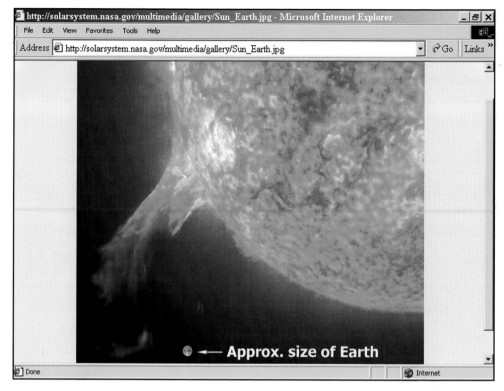

http://solarsystem.nasa.gov/multimedia/gallery/Sun_Earth.jpg - Microsoft Internet Explorer

File   Edit   View   Favorites   Tools   Help

Address http://solarsystem.nasa.gov/multimedia/gallery/Sun_Earth.jpg   Go   Links

⊙ ⟵ **Approx. size of Earth**

Done   Internet

🔺 *Another violent eruption of material from the Sun into space is known as a coronal mass ejection, or CME. Here, the enormous size of a CME is evident when compared with a much smaller body representing Earth.*

in areas of the photosphere where there is a strong concentration of magnetic fields. Sunspots appear darker than the rest of the Sun's surface because the magnetic forces disrupt the movement of hot gas, and thus of energy, to the surface. Because the flow of energy is interrupted, the sunspots are 2,500°F to 3,600°F (1,371°C to 1,982°C) cooler than the surrounding areas.

At sunset, the larger sunspots are visible to the naked eye, but no one should try to look at the Sun without using special solar filters designed for viewing the Sun. (Sunglasses and homemade filters do not protect the human eye from the partial or total blindness that can result from even a few seconds of unfiltered sunlight.)

People have, however, observed sunspots for thousands of years. Ancient Chinese astronomers, who viewed the Sun through thick clouds or when it rose or set, began keeping written records of their observations of sunspots as early as 600 B.C. Toward the end of the year 1610, Galileo Galilei and other astronomers were able to see sunspots through the newly invented instrument known as the telescope. Galileo used his observations to measure the rotation of the Sun and to prove that its surface changes in appearance as the spots come and go. In 1843, German astronomer Heinrich Schwabe discovered that sunspots occur in cycles, with the largest number appearing, on average, every eleven years.

There are other kinds of intense and violent activities taking place on the Sun. Hot ionized gases and magnetic fields rising from the Sun's surface result in spicules, solar flares, prominences, and coronal mass ejections (CMEs), all which may be different parts of the same phenomenon. Spicules are jetlike spikes of upward-moving gas that rise from the Sun's photosphere thousands of miles through the chromosphere and into the corona. Prominences and solar flares also extend from the photosphere into the Sun's upper atmosphere. They are associated with sunspots, and such solar activity reaches a peak at the height of the eleven-year sunspot cycle. Prominences are condensed clouds of solar gas that erupt from the Sun's surface and are bent and twisted by magnetic fields into an arch. Most prominences loop back to the Sun's surface, but some fly off into space. Prominences are often more than thousands of miles long and up to 3,000 miles (4,827 kilometers) thick. Some prominences rise and fall in just a few hours, although others can last for weeks.

Solar Flares and CMEs

A solar flare is an even stronger eruption, which results in charged particles in the upper atmosphere of the Sun becoming intensely bright. Flares can reach temperatures of 9,000,000°F (5,000,000°C). Flares usually last just a few minutes, but in that

The northern lights over Colorado. These bright lights in Earth's skies are produced by the interaction between charged particles from the Sun and gas molecules in Earth's atmosphere.

short time they can release energy equal to the explosion of 10 million hydrogen bombs.

From time to time, huge bubbles of material are ejected from the corona into space. These coronal mass ejections can contain as much as 50 billion tons (45 billion metric tons) of ionized gas. Such coronal mass ejections are associated with solar flares and prominences. When material and magnetic fields from solar flares and coronal mass ejections reach Earth, they can damage satellites, disrupt communications, and produce power surges on electrical transmission lines. But such geomagnetic storms also produce beautiful displays of the aurora, the northern and southern lights. The charged particles from the Sun interact with molecules of gas in the upper atmosphere above Earth's north and south magnetic poles. This causes the gas molecules to glow, resulting in swirling rays and curtains of colored light.

Chapter 3

Movements of the Sun

All of the solar system's planets, asteroids, and comets orbit the Sun, the center of the solar system. But although the Sun seems stationary in relation to the various bodies revolving around it, it has movements of its own.

▶ The Sun's Orbit and Rotation

The Sun is located about two thirds of the way from the center of the Milky Way galaxy, in one of the galaxy's spiral arms. The Sun's

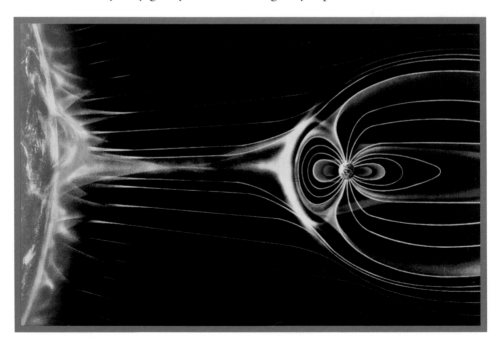

△ This diagram illustrates the flow of magnetism between the Sun, pictured with its violent magnetic disturbances, and Earth. Scientists say that magnetism is the key to understanding the Sun.

distance from the center of the galaxy is about thirty thousand light-years. Just as the inner planets in our solar system revolve around the Sun more rapidly than the outer planets, the stars closer to the galactic center orbit around it more quickly than the stars farther out from the center. The Sun moves around the galactic center at a speed of 721,800 feet per second (220,005 meters per second), carrying all the bodies of the solar system along with it. At this speed, it takes the Sun 240 million years to complete one trip around the galactic center. So far, the Sun has orbited the Milky Way galaxy more than nineteen times during its 4.5-billion-year lifetime.

Rotating at Different Speeds

In 1610, Galileo used his telescope to project sunspot patterns onto a paper screen. The shifting motion of the sunspots proved to him that the Sun rotates on its axis. The English astronomer Edmond Halley (1656–1742) also made extensive observations of sunspot activity. Halley determined that the Sun near its equator makes one rotation in twenty-five days. Nearer to its poles, the Sun takes nearly thirty-five days to rotate once.[1] Like Earth, the Sun rotates from west to east. Unlike Earth, a solid body with one uniform speed of rotation, the Sun has different speeds of rotation depending on the latitude of a particular part of the surface. So the Sun is said to have differential rotation, where Earth has solid-body rotation. If one part of Earth were to suddenly rotate at a different rate than the rest of the planet, Earth would be ripped apart. But because the Sun is made of gas, it does not rotate rigidly.

Further complicating the picture, scientists have determined that gases deep within the Sun's interior rotate at a uniform speed from pole to pole. Some scientists believe that the forces generated by the contrasting speeds of rotation may create the Sun's magnetic field.[2]

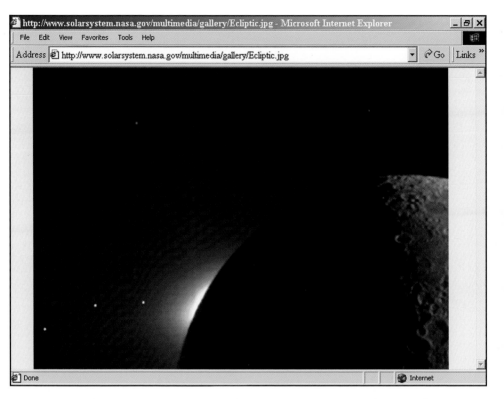

http://www.solarsystem.nasa.gov/multimedia/gallery/Ecliptic.jpg - Microsoft Internet Explorer

File   Edit   View   Favorites   Tools   Help

Address 🔊 http://www.solarsystem.nasa.gov/multimedia/gallery/Ecliptic.jpg   ▼ ⟳Go ‖Links ⁀

🔊 Done   🌐 Internet

▲ *The ecliptic plane is an imaginary plane that contains Earth's orbit around the Sun. This photograph is a remarkable illustration of that plane. Pictured, from right to left, are the Moon lit by Earth's reflection, the rising of the Sun's corona over the dark part of the Moon, and the planets Saturn, Mars, and Mercury.*

▷ Solar Eclipses

As the Moon revolves around Earth, it comes between Earth and the Sun nearly every six months, causing a partial solar eclipse. On rare occasions, the center of the Moon passes directly in front of the center of the Sun. This is known as a total solar eclipse. The Moon's shadow traces a path across part of Earth's surface. People living in the path of the eclipse watch the sky grow dark as the Moon moves in front of the Sun. Those living near the path of the total eclipse see a partial solar eclipse.

During a total solar eclipse, the time in which the Sun is completely blocked in a particular location can last from a few seconds

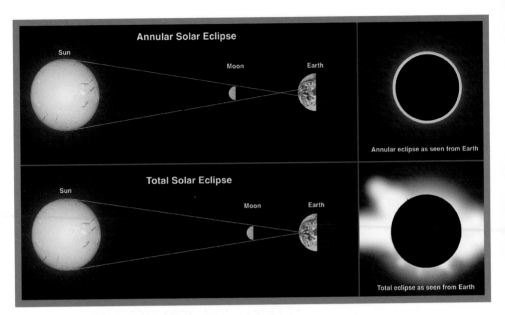

Annular Solar Eclipse

Sun   Moon   Earth

Annular eclipse as seen from Earth

Total Solar Eclipse

Sun   Moon   Earth

Total eclipse as seen from Earth

▲ *In an annular eclipse, the Moon, at its farthest point from Earth, appears to be too small to hide the Sun, so an annulus, or ring, of the Sun is seen around the dark body of the Moon. During a total solar eclipse, the Moon is perfectly aligned between Earth and the Sun.*

to seven and a half minutes. Usually two, and rarely five, partial solar eclipses occur each year. A total solar eclipse occurs only about once every three hundred years as seen from any one location because the Moon's shadow falls over only a small part of Earth in one eclipse.

For thousands of years, solar eclipses often inspired fear and terror. In many places, people were afraid that once the Sun disappeared, it would never reappear. People in many different cultures around the world created their own myths and legends to explain the phenomenon. Often, the disappearance of the Sun was a sign that the Sun god was either angry, sad, sick, or neglectful. In some places, solar eclipses were associated with the outbreak of epidemics. Some cultures saw a solar eclipse as a lover's quarrel between the Sun and the Moon. In many ancient cultures, a solar eclipse was seen as a battle between the Sun and spirits of darkness, or a monster's attempt to destroy the Sun. In ancient Egypt, people believed that a serpent from the Underworld ate the Sun god as it sailed across the sky in its boat. In ancient China, it was a heavenly dog who ate the Sun.[3]

Although superstitions about eclipses continued through the ages, there were people thousands of years ago who began to understand the true nature of eclipses. Babylonian astronomers were keeping careful records of eclipses as early as 700 B.C. In the fifth century B.C., the Greek historian Herodotus wrote that the Greek mathematician Thales of Miletus had predicted a solar eclipse would occur in the year 585 B.C. The eclipse did take place that year during a battle between the Lydians and Medes of Asia Minor. This particular eclipse had a beneficial effect. Apparently, the soldiers on both sides were so frightened by the eclipse that they stopped fighting and signed a peace treaty, ending five years of war. Thales is often given credit for being the first person to successfully predict a solar eclipse. However, he did not give an actual date but merely suggested the year in which a solar eclipse would occur. More than two thousand years would pass before the English astronomer Edmond Halley became the first person to make truly accurate predictions of solar eclipses.[4]

The Birth and Death of the Sun

The Sun, the giver of life to the inhabitants of Earth, cannot shine forever. It will eventually use up the hydrogen fuel in its core. Just as living organisms are born and die, all stars, including the Sun, go through a cycle of birth, life, and death. The eventual death of the Sun will be preceded by the end of all life on Earth—and possibly the end of Earth itself.

▶ How the Sun Was Formed

The Sun formed about 4.6 billion years ago. A cloud of dust and hydrogen gas particles swirling in the space between the stars became dense enough to heat up. The dust and gas collapsed under their own gravity and the cloud, called a solar nebula, began to rotate and flatten into what scientists call an "accretion disk."[1] This idea for the origin of the Sun was first proposed in the eighteenth century by the German philosopher Immanuel Kant. But it was a French physicist

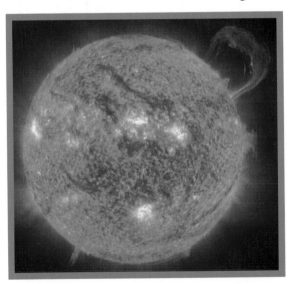

◀ *The telescope aboard the SOHO spacecraft produced this image of a huge handle-shaped prominence erupting from the Sun. The hottest spots on this image are those that appear nearly white, while the coolest spots are the darkest red.*

▲ *Billions of years from now, the Sun, a star, will grow even hotter and brighter than it is now.*

named Pierre Simon Laplace who developed Kant's idea into a scientific theory.

The center of the disk began to glow as it grew hotter and denser. At this stage, the center of the disk, which contained most of the mass, was not yet a star, but a protostar. As soon as the pro- tostar became dense and hot enough, the nuclear fusion process could begin, and a star was born. Shortly after the Sun formed at the center of the disk, the planets of the solar system formed from the debris that circled the Sun.

Since the Sun formed, it has gradually grown larger and brighter. It is now 30 percent brighter than it was 4.5 billion years ago. By now, the Sun has used up about 37 percent of its hydro- gen fuel, converting it into helium. The remaining hydrogen will last about another 5 billion years.

The Sun Becomes a Red Giant

The Sun, classified as an average star, will follow the life cycle typ- ical of such stars. Scientists can understand this life cycle from having observed millions of other similar stars in various stages of the cycle.

Over the next 5 billion years, the Sun will grow hotter and brighter, eventually becoming a huge red-giant star. As the hydro- gen in the core is used up, the core will slowly collapse and heat up. This will cause the outer layers of the Sun to expand. The outer layers will cool as they expand, resulting in the reddish color. The planet Mercury will be swallowed up as the Sun becomes 170 times larger than it is today.

At this time the Sun will be 2,300 times brighter than it is now. If any people or other creatures were still alive on Earth, they would see a Sun that filled the whole daytime sky. But by this time, Earth would have become too hot for any forms of life to exist, except possibly bacteria. In about 3 billion years, Earth's oceans will have boiled away, and Earth's surface will have melted.

▲ *As the Sun nears the end of its life, with it fuel sources spent, its outer layers will be thrown into space. Scientists think that those layers may form a beautiful planetary nebula, perhaps like the Dumbbell Nebula pictured.*

▷ From Red Giant to White Dwarf to Black Dwarf

In about 5 billion years, the Sun's hydrogen fuel will be used up. The core of the Sun will contract and become much hotter—hot enough to burn helium. As the helium becomes used up, the core will contract again, but nuclear processes will continue as helium fuses into carbon, producing enough energy to stop the contraction. But carbon cannot become fusion fuel for the Sun as it can for bigger stars. So eventually, in about 50 million to 100 million years, the Sun's fuel sources will be gone. As the carbon burns in its final stages, however, the Sun's outer layers will be driven into

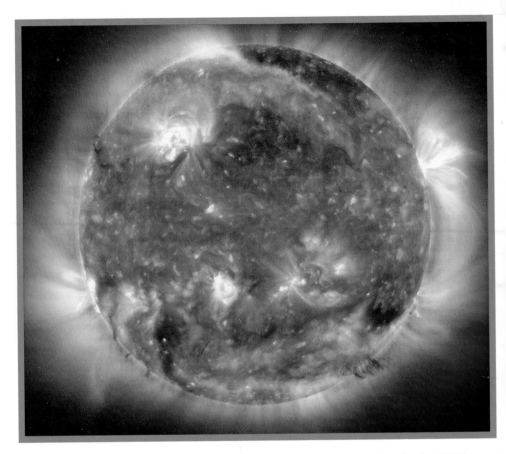

▲ *In this remarkable photograph, separate images of the Sun taken by the SOHO telescope have been combined and colorized to reveal solar features.*

space, where they will probably form a beautiful planetary nebula, a mass of starry dust and gas.

The sun's core will collapse into a white dwarf star, a white-hot ball of super-dense matter no larger than Earth. Since the Sun will no longer have any source of fuel, it can no longer sustain nuclear reactions. Scientists believe that the Sun will gradually cool down, eventually lose all its heat, and become a cold, dense, dark star known as a black dwarf.

Scientists Study the Sun

We have come a long way in our understanding of the Sun since we began observing and wondering about it thousands of years ago. But we still have much to learn.

▶ Telescopes

Since Galileo's time, the telescope has been a valuable tool for making scientific observations of the Sun. Today, telescopes are still extremely important, especially those that are mounted in spacecraft orbiting Earth and orbiting the Sun. Solar observatories on Earth, such as the Mauna Loa Solar Observatory in Hawaii, have special solar telescopes designed for viewing the Sun. One of these is called a coronagraph, used for viewing the Sun's corona. Until 1930, scientists were able to observe the corona only during a solar eclipse. But that year, Bernard Lyot fitted a telescope with a small circular plate that covered the solar disk just as the Moon would. So the coronagraph allows scientists to study the Sun's corona on any clear day, without having to wait for an eclipse.

Scientists also use radio telescopes to study the Sun. Whereas optical telescopes operate in the visible part of the Sun's electromagnetic spectrum, radio telescopes provide data obtained from the Sun's invisible radio waves. Because radio waves are thousands of times longer than visible-light waves, a radio telescope would have to be hundreds or thousands of feet wide to provide sharp images. Instead, an array of many dishes are linked together electronically, such as the twenty-seven dishes of the Very Large Array (VLA) at Socorro, New Mexico. Such an array of dishes is called a radioheliograph.[1]

The address bar of the browser window reads:

http://www.solarsystem.nasa.gov/multimedia/gallery/Guerra7.jpg - Microsoft Internet Explorer

File   Edit   View   Favorites   Tools   Help

Address 🔲 http://www.solarsystem.nasa.gov/multimedia/gallery/Guerra7.jpg   ▼ ∂Go Links »

▲ *The Sun continues to fascinate us on Earth. Here, a photograph captures a partial solar eclipse as seen from Texas in 2004.*

▶ Analyzing Sunlight

In addition to using telescopes, there are other important methods for learning about the Sun. In 1666, Sir Isaac Newton focused a beam of sunlight through a glass prism. He discovered that the prism split the sunlight into separate colors, called a spectrum. He observed that the different colors were bent by different amounts in the prism, according to their respective wavelengths. So he concluded that white light is a combination of different colors. This discovery would lead to the development of spectroscopy, a method of analyzing sunlight.

In 1802, the English physicist William H. Wollaston noticed that there were many fine dark lines in the Sun's spectrum. In

1814, the German physicist Joseph von Fraunhofer used an instrument known as a spectrograph to study the solar spectrum. A spectrograph measures the wavelength of each feature, or "line" in the spectrum. Fraunhofer produced a chart of the Sun's spectrum showing hundreds of dark lines.[2] Fraunhofer did not know what these lines were, but he labeled and recorded them.

In 1859, the German chemist Gustav Kirchhoff and his coworker Robert Bunsen discovered that Fraunhofer's spectral lines were produced from absorption of light by chemical elements present in the Sun's chromosphere.[3] They discovered that each chemical has its own pattern of lines. By comparing the solar spectrum with the spectra of vaporized chemical elements in the

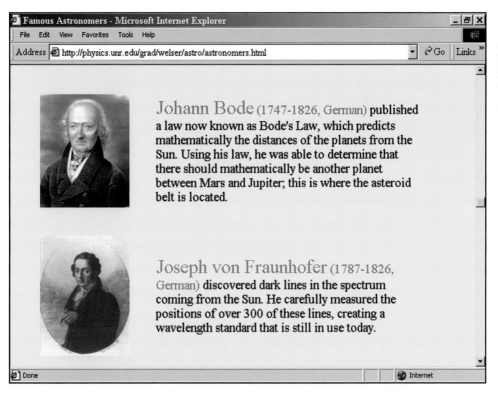

Famous Astronomers - Microsoft Internet Explorer

File   Edit   View   Favorites   Tools   Help

Address http://physics.unr.edu/grad/welser/astro/astronomers.html   Go   Links

Johann Bode (1747-1826, German) published a law now known as Bode's Law, which predicts mathematically the distances of the planets from the Sun. Using his law, he was able to determine that there should mathematically be another planet between Mars and Jupiter; this is where the asteroid belt is located.

Joseph von Fraunhofer (1787-1826, German) discovered dark lines in the spectrum coming from the Sun. He carefully measured the positions of over 300 of these lines, creating a wavelength standard that is still in use today.

Done   Internet

△ Two German scientists of the eighteenth century advanced our knowledge of the Sun. Johann Bode came up with a mathematical law to predict the distances of the planets from the Sun. Joseph von Fraunhofer used an instrument to measure the wavelength of the solar spectrum.

laboratory, it was possible to identify the different chemicals in the gases of the Sun. In 1885, a Swiss mathematician and school-teacher named Johann Jakob Balmer determined that the Sun is mainly made of hydrogen.

Using the spectrograph, scientists have been able to identify the chemical composition of the Sun. Another instrument called a spectroheliograph allows scientists to focus on a single particular wavelength of sunlight at a time.

Observing the Sun From Space

Studying the Sun from space offers obvious advantages for Earth-bound astronomers. Depending where orbiting spacecraft are placed, the Sun can be observed 24 hours a day, 365 days a year. And in space there are no atmospheric conditions to interfere with the view. In the 1960s, the National Aeronautics and Space Administration (NASA) launched a series of eight spacecraft called Orbiting Solar Observatories (OSOs). The OSOs carried out solar observations until 1979, studying the Sun's ultraviolet, gamma, and X-rays throughout an eleven-year sunspot cycle. But the OSOs carried small telescopes and could not produce sharp images of the Sun.

In 1973, NASA launched Skylab, the first American orbital space station. One of the main tasks of the astronauts on board was to study the Sun from space. The Apollo Telescope Mount (ATM) on Skylab was the world's first large solar observatory in space. The ATM included a coronagraph, several spectrographs, and two X-ray telescopes to study X-rays given off by the Sun. Between 1973 and 1974, the astronauts on Skylab took more than 150,000 images of the Sun. Skylab orbited Earth until 1979, when it reentered the atmosphere. The following year, NASA launched the Solar Maximum Mission (SMM), also known as SolarMax, to study solar flares and the Sun during the most active part of the sunspot cycle.

△ *The launch of the eighth and final Orbiting Solar Observatory mission.*

In 1990, NASA and the European Space Agency (ESA) launched the *Ulysses* space probe to explore the environment over the Sun's poles. In November 1994, *Ulysses* completed its first pass over the Sun's south pole. *Ulysses* sent back data indicating that the Sun has a uniform magnetic field rather than solar magnetic poles and that the solar wind in the southern polar region is blowing at about 2 million miles per hour (3 million kilometers per hour).

SOHO, TRACE, and RHESSI: Targeting the Sun

In 1995, NASA and ESA launched the Solar and Heliospheric Observatory (SOHO). This solar-orbiting spacecraft's mission is to study the structure of the Sun's interior, to learn what causes the incredibly hot temperatures of the solar corona, and to determine where the solar wind originates. The scientific technique for studying the Sun's interior is known as helioseismology, just as seismology is a study of tremors inside Earth.

SOHO scientists have detected sound waves in the Sun that are caused by the churning of gases in the convective layer. The sound waves cause ripples on the Sun's surface, so SOHO can measure the waves by observing the ripples. By studying the sound waves and their echoes, it is possible to determine the temperatures of

◁ *An artist's conception of the Solar and Heliospheric Observatory. This spacecraft that orbits the Sun has produced information for scientists that may some day help them to predict solar eruptions.*

regions inside the Sun that the sound waves pass through. It is also possible to detect solar storms occurring on the far side of the Sun, the side facing away from Earth, because such storms cause sound waves. This information can help scientists forecast solar eruptions such as coronal mass ejections.

Making such predictions and determining how and when Earth will feel the effects of solar activity is a relatively new science known as space weather. Knowing when a large burst of solar particles is headed our way may prevent astronauts in space from being exposed to harmful radiation. It may also allow us to protect orbiting satellites from harmful solar activity.

In 1998, NASA launched TRACE (Transition Region and Coronal Explorer). Working with SOHO, TRACE makes observations of the Sun's magnetic fields as they emerge from deep inside the Sun through all of the star's outer layers. In 2002, NASA launched RHESSI (Reuven Ramaty High Energy Solar Spectroscopic Imager) to study the release of energy in solar flares. This space mission was the first to be named after a NASA scientist. Dr. Reuven Ramaty was a pioneering researcher in the field of solar physics.

The Future

NASA has more missions planned for the future to learn more about the Sun. The Solar TErrestrial RElations Observatory (STEREO) is scheduled for launch in 2005. It includes two solar-orbiting satellites and will give scientists a three-dimensional view of coronal mass ejections. The Solar Dynamics Observatory (SDO), scheduled for launch in 2008, will make a more complete study of the Sun's interior. Scientists hope the SDO will enable them to predict sunspots before they occur. Next, the Solar Probe will be a mission of exploration and discovery, the first spacecraft to fly through the Sun's corona. It will study how the solar wind is driven by energy flowing into the solar atmosphere.

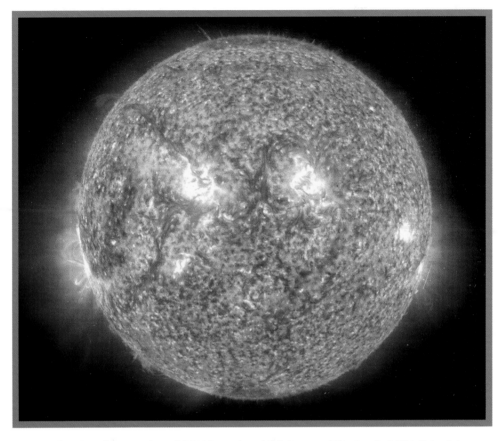

▲ *The telescope aboard SOHO produced this image of the Sun in 2004. Scientists are learning more about Earth's closest star—and giver of life—every day.*

Although scientists are learning more about the Sun every day, many mysteries remain. Among other things, scientists hope to understand what causes the eleven-year sunspot cycle, what makes the corona so hot, and how big solar flares can get. As our methods for investigating the Sun advance, and our instruments become more sophisticated, we will eventually uncover the secrets of the Sun.

Glossary

chromosphere—The fiery red layer of the Sun that lies above the photosphere.

convective zone—The region or layer outside the radiative zone of the Sun that extends to the Sun's visible surface.

corona—The outer atmosphere of the Sun, which can be seen during a total solar eclipse.

coronal mass ejection—Large bubbles of material that are ejected from the Sun's corona into space.

electromagnetic spectrum—Radiation that travels and spreads out.

opaque—Blocking the passage of radiant energy and light.

photosphere—The visible surface of the Sun, which consists of a very thin layer of gas.

prominences—Condensed clouds of solar gas that erupt from the Sun's surface and are often more than 1,000 miles (1,609 kilometers) long.

radiative zone—The region or layer surrounding the Sun's core.

solar eclipse—The passage of the Moon directly between the Sun and the Earth, which casts the Moon's shadow on Earth and blocks out either part of the Sun, in a partial solar eclipse, or all of the Sun, in a total solar eclipse.

solar flares—Massive gas bubbles that erupt from the Sun's corona.

spectroscopy—The study of spectral lines (light that is given off at a specific frequency by an atom or molecule). Such study allows scientists to learn the chemical composition of stars, gas, or dust.

spicules—Spikes of gas that rise from the Sun's photosphere through the chromosphere and into the corona.

sunspots—Huge dark spots on the Sun's surface caused by magnetic disturbances in the photosphere.

thermonuclear fusion—A process in which the nuclei of hydrogen and helium atoms, when subjected to a high temperature, combine and release energy. This process is the power source at the Sun's core.

Chapter 1. The Closest Star

1. Robert W. Noyes, *The Sun, Our Star* (Cambridge, Mass.: Harvard University Press, 1982), p. 8.

2. Owen Gingerich, "Great Revelations," in *Fire of Life, The Smithsonian Book of the Sun* (New York: W. W. Norton & Company, 1981), p. 30.

3. Mark Littmann, Ken Willcox, and Fred Espenak, *Totality: Eclipses of the Sun* (New York: Oxford University Press, 1999), pp. 30–31.

Chapter 2. A Gigantic Nuclear Furnace

1. Mark Littmann, Ken Willcox, and Fred Espenak, *Totality: Eclipses of the Sun* (New York: Oxford University Press, 1999), p. 54.

2. Leon Golub and Jay M. Pasachoff, *Nearest Star: The Surprising Science of Our Sun* (Cambridge, Mass.: Harvard University Press, 2001), p. 12.

3. Thomas R. Watters, *Planets: A Smithsonian Guide* (New York: Macmillan, 1995), p. 36.

4. Robert W. Noyes, *The Sun, Our Star* (Cambridge, Mass.: Harvard University Press, 1982), p. 48.

5. Littmann, Willcox, and Espenak, p. 57.

Chapter 3. Movements of the Sun

1. Duncan Steel, *Eclipse* (Washington, D.C.: Joseph Henry Press, 2001), p. 169.

2. Kenneth R. Lang, *The Cambridge Encyclopedia of the Sun* (Cambridge, England: Cambridge University Press, 2001), p. 88.

3. Mark Littmann, Ken Willcox, and Fred Espenak, *Totality: Eclipses of the Sun* (New York: Oxford University Press, 1999), p. 41.

4. Steel, pp. 86–89.

Chapter 4. The Birth and Death of the Sun

1. Peter D. Ward and Donald Brownlee, *The Life and Death of Planet Earth* (New York: Henry Holt and Company, 2003), p. 26.

Chapter 5. Scientists Study the Sun

1. Leon Golub and Jay M. Pasachoff, *Nearest Star: The Surprising Science of Our Sun* (Cambridge, Mass.: Harvard University Press, 2001), p. 17.

2. Ibid., p. 21.

3. Robert W. Noyes, *The Sun, Our Star* (Cambridge, Mass.: Harvard University Press, 1982), p. 31.

Asimov, Isaac, with revisions and updating by Richard Hantula. *The Sun*. Milwaukee: Gareth Stevens Publishing, 2002.

Bell, Trudy E. *The Sun: Our Nearest Star*. North Mankato, Minn.: Smart Apple Media, 2003.

Cole, Michael D. *The Sun—The Center of the Solar System*. Berkeley Heights, N.J.: Enslow Publishers, Inc., 2001.

Gallant, Roy A. *The Life Stories of Stars*. New York: Benchmark Books, 2000.

Kosek, Jane Kelly. *What's Inside the Sun?* New York: The Rosen Publishing Group, Inc., 1999.

Miller, Ron. *The Sun*. Brookfield, Conn.: Twenty-First Century Books, 2002.

Ride, Sally, and Tam O'Shaughnessy. *Exploring Our Solar System*. New York: Crown Publishers, 2003.

Ridpath, Ian. *Facts on File Stars and Planets Atlas*. New York: Facts on File, 2001.

Schwabacher, Martin. *The Sun*. New York: Benchmark Books, 2003.

Silverstein, Alvin, Virginia Silverstein, and Laura Silverstein Nunn. *The Universe*. Brookfield, Conn.: Twenty-First Century Books, 2003.

Spangenburg, Ray, and Kit Moser. *The Life and Death of Stars*. New York: Franklin Watts, 2003.